D0064598

Shabba me whiskers! Andy Stanton's *Mr Gum* is winner of the Roald Dahl Funny Prize, the Red House Children's Book Award AND the Blue Peter Book Award for The Most Fun Story With Pictures. AND he's been shortlisted for LOADS of other prizes too! It's barking bonkers!

PRAISE FOR *Mr Gum*:

'Do not even think about buying another book – This is gut-spillingly funny.' Alex, aged 13

'It's hilarious, it's brilliant... Stanton's the Guv'nor, The Boss.' Danny Baker, BBC London Radio

'Funniest book I have ever and will ever read... When I read this to my mum she burst out laughing and nearly wet herself ... When I had finished the book I wanted to read it all over again it was so good.' Bryony, aged 8

'Funny? You bet.' Guardian

'Andy Stanton accumulates silliness and jokes in an irresistible, laughter-inducing romp.' Sunday Times

'Raucous, revoltingly rambunctious and nose-snortingly funny.' Daily Mail

'David Tazzyman's illustrations match the irreverent sparks of word wizardry with slapdash delight.' Junior Education

'This is weird, wacky and one in a million.' Primary Times

'It provoked long and painful belly laughs from my daughter, who is eight.' Daily Telegraph

'As always, Stanton has a ball with dialogue, detail and devilish plot twists.' Scotsman

'We laughed so much it hurt.' Sophie, aged 9

'You will laugh so much you'll ache in places you didn't know you had.' First News

'A riotous read.' Sunday Express

'It's utterly bonkers and then a bit more - you'll love every madcap moment.' TBK Magazine

'Chaotically crazy.' Jewish Chronicle

'Designed to tickle young funny bones.' Glasgow Herald

'A complete joy to read whatever your age.'
This is Kids' Stuff

'The truth is a lemon meringue!' Friday O'Leary

'They are brilliant.' Zoe Ball, Radio 2

'Smooky palooki! This book is well brilliant.' Jeremy Strong

For Tom Ralis and his class at Cherry Orchard Primary

EGMONT

We bring stories to life

Mr Gum and the Goblins
First published 2007 by Egmont UK Limited, 239 Kensington High Street London W8 6SA

Text copyright © 2007 Andy Stanton
Illustration copyright © 2007 David Tazzyman

The moral rights of the author and illustrator have been asserted

ISBN 978 1 4052 2816 9

11

www.egmont.co.uk/mrgum

A CIP catalogue record for this title is available from the British Library

Printed and bound in Great Britain by the CPI Group

MIX
Paper from
responsible sources
FSC® C018306

Egmont is passionate about helping to preserve the world's remaining ancient forests. We only use paper from legal and sustainable forest sources, so we know where every single tree comes from that goes into every paper that makes up every book.

This book is made from paper certified by the Forestry Stewardship Council (FSC), an organisation dedicated to promoting responsible management of forest resources. For more information on the FSC, please visit **www.fsc.org**. To learn more about Egmont's sustainable paper policy, please visit **www.egmont.co.uk/ethical**.

Mr Gum

and the
Goblins

Andy Stanton

Illustrated by
David Tazzyman

Meet some of the townsfolk of Lamonic Bibber

Mrs Lovely

Friday O'Leary

Billy William the Third

Old Granny

Mr Gum

Alan Taylor

Polly

Martin Launderette

Contents

Chapter 1

In The Dead Of Winter

It was the Dead Of Winter and the little town of Lamonic Bibber lay under a blanket of snow and ice. Everywhere you looked, there was snow and ice. On the trees – snow and ice. On the ground – snow and ice. Inside the Museum of Snow and Ice – snow and ice. It was the coldest winter anyone could remember.

Inside the inns and taverns the men folk sat around blazing log fires, drinking their ale and telling stories of never-to-be-forgotten heroes like Whatsisname and That Tall Man In The Shirt Who Killed All Those Dragons. In the houses, mothers put their young ones to bed, soothing them with gentle lullabies about fierce lions and crocodiles. In a little cottage by the meadow, a hobbit sat reading *The Lord of the Rings* and

microwaving his feet to keep warm. 'Twas the Dead Of Winter, all right.

The streets of Lamonic Bibber were quiet at that late hour but presently there came the sound of footsteps as three shadowy figures turned into the high street. And now I will tell you who they were, for I have seen them before – and perhaps you know them too.

The leader was Friday O'Leary, a wise old man who knew the secrets of Time and Space.

He carried a lantern which cast a ghostly yellow light on the icy cobblestones. Next came a nine-year-old girl called Polly. She too carried a lantern and it shone brave and true, just like her pure strong heart. And last of all came little Alan Taylor, the Headmaster of 𝕾𝖆𝖎𝖓𝖙 𝕻𝖙𝖊𝖗𝖔𝖉𝖆𝖈𝖙𝖞𝖑'𝖘 𝕾𝖈𝖍𝖔𝖔𝖑 𝕱𝖔𝖗 𝕿𝖍𝖊 𝕻𝖔𝖔𝖗. He was a gingerbread man with electric muscles and he was only 15.24 centimetres tall. Alan Taylor was far too small to carry a lantern, but he had coated an acorn in glow-in-the-dark paint and that was almost as good.

"'Tis late, friends,' whispered Friday O'Leary as the church bells rang for ten o'clock, belting out like absolute marshmallows in the wintry night. 'We should be getting home, for who knows what strange spirits are about in the Dead Of Winter?'

'There are no strange spirits, kind Friday,' chuckled Alan Taylor. 'Methinks you have been spending too much time in the taverns, listening to the idle tales of drunken fools!'

'Hey,' said Polly. 'Why's everyone a-talkin' all funny like in weird old books? We only done came out to gets a takeaway kebab.'

But just then a horrible wailing noise rose on the wind like an out-of-tune opera singer being dragged down a blackboard. Polly and Alan Taylor jumped in fright and Friday did a dozen press-ups in terror.

'WURP!' he trembled. 'What was that?'

'I gots no idea,' gulped Polly. 'But I don't likes the sound of that sound one little bit.'

'What if . . .' squeaked Alan Taylor, bravely weeing himself in fear. 'What if it's Mr Gum?'

Now, at the mention of that name they all went very quiet, because there was nothing worse than Mr Gum, not even accidentally falling into a volcano full of history teachers. For Mr Gum and his no-good friend Billy William the Third were the worst criminals Lamonic Bibber had ever seen. And they had done some of the most shocking things of all time, including:

1. Trying to poison a massive whopper of a dog called Jake to death and destruction
2. Trying to steal a billion pounds off poor little Alan Taylor
3. Tons of other stuff I can't think of at the moment

'But Alan Taylor, no one's seen Mr Gum for ages,' said Polly.

'Nonetheless, he might have come back,' replied Friday gravely. 'For as the famous saying goes – "*He might have come back.*" Let us investigate!'

And the three friends set off to see what was what, their lanterns swinging hopefully against the darkness. With each step they took the wailing grew louder, until –

WAAAAIIIILLLL

'It's coming from the alley behind Mrs Lovely's sweetshop,' said Friday, and even as he said those words, a hunched-up figure appeared in the narrow passage, staggering towards them with outstretched arms like a mummy. Not the nice type of mummy, obviously. The type with dusty old bandages who's always chasing you through museums at night because you dug them up out of their pyramid because you were a scientist and that's what scientists do.

'But hold on,' frowned Polly. 'We haven't been messin' around in no pyramids lately. That can't be a mummy after all. Why,' she exclaimed, 'it's Mrs Lovely! An' she's been all duffed up an' mangled!'

'NO!' cried Friday in distress, for Mrs Lovely was his wife and he loved her like a barbecue. *'NO!'* he cried into the cold, cold night. *'NOOOO!'*

Chapter 2
Talk of the Devil

But alas, it was indeed Mrs Lovely, owner of the sweetshop and general all-round goodie. Onwards she came, stumbling half-blind over empty pizza boxes and wailing miserably all the while. At once, Friday ran up to offer her aid and comfort and some hazelnuts – and she

collapsed unconscious in his arms. It was very dramatic and everything.

'What happened to thee?' Friday sobbed, clutching Mrs Lovely to his ear. 'What badness has befallen thee, oh darling wife?'

'Save your questions, Friday,' advised Alan Taylor. 'Mrs Lovely is in shock and it will take more than hazelnuts before she can tell us her terrible story. Come, let us get her to a place of rest.'

So together the heroes carried Mrs Lovely to a nearby inn. A sign over the door read:

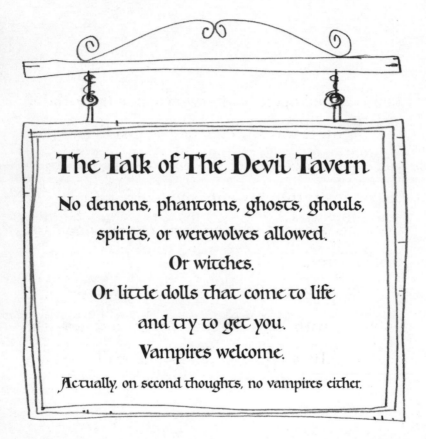

The Talk of The Devil Tavern

No demons, phantoms, ghosts, ghouls,
spirits, or werewolves allowed.
Or witches.
Or little dolls that come to life
and try to get you.
Vampires welcome.

Actually, on second thoughts, no vampires either.

Polly pushed open the heavy wooden door and in they went. It was warm and cosy inside and they were glad to be out of the cold – but upon their entry everything went suddenly quiet. The men folk stopped singing their merry songs and looked afraid.

'DEMONS!' cried one, starting up and pointing with a trembling finger towards the visitors. "Tis a horde of demons come to eat our bones!'

'You're right, Jack!' shrieked another. ''Tis demons for sure!'

And at that, the men folk flew into a panic, hiding under chairs, under tables, in pints of beer – anywhere they could. One man disguised himself as a fruit machine and stood there in the corner covered in cherries and coughing up pound coins.

'Blimey, you men folk is well ignorant,' said Polly indignantly. 'We're not demons.'

'Not even slightly?' asked one of the men folk anxiously.

'No,' said Polly firmly. 'You lot's drunk too much beer an' it's turned your brains all fuzzy an' full of bad 'maginations. Now go home, men folk, an' get some sleep. An' don't blame me if you all gots terrible headaches in the mornin', I shouldn't wonder.'

'OK, nine-year-old girl,' said the men folk, 'you're the boss, for some reason.' And off home they went.

🐝 🐝 🐝

'I do apologise about all that demon talk,' said the Innkeeper, as he led Polly and her friends upstairs. 'But though they were drunk, the men folk were right to be afraid. You never know WHO's going to come through the door in this terrible season, when spirits and ghouls are at large. Why, only last week an evil skeleton came in and did a poo on the carpet. How I hate the Dead Of Winter!' he exclaimed. And the Innkeeper showed the heroes to a cosy little bedroom with wooden floorboards, bowed once and disappeared back downstairs.

With great care, Friday dumped Mrs Lovely down on the little bed. Polly fetched a flannel and gently she scrubbed the slime from Mrs Lovely's goodly face. And Alan Taylor hopped up on to her chin and gently he flossed her goodly teeth.

'I shall take first watch,' said Friday, pulling up a chair. 'If she wakes I will wake you too. But until then, she must not be disturbed.

THE TRUTH IS A LEMON MERINGUE!' he yelled at the top of his lungs, as he sometimes liked to do.

At once Mrs Lovely's eyes snapped open and she sat bolt upright in bed like a startled panda caught shoplifting bamboo.

'Whaa? Eh? Boing?!' she gabbled, looking around in confusion. 'Where am I?'

'Fear not, Mrs L,' exclaimed Friday, 'For 'tis I, your beloved husband, me.'

'Oh, hello, Friday,' said Mrs Lovely weakly. 'What's going on?'

But suddenly she caught her breath and drew the bedcover to her cheek in terror.

'Goblin Mountain!' she murmured in the flickering candlelight. 'Now I remember!'

'Tell us your tale, dearest wife-face,' said Friday, tenderly clasping her nose to his. 'But will you do it as a song?' he asked eagerly.

'Now is not the time for songs, my love,'

replied Mrs Lovely. 'Besides, I'm all weak and feeble. I'm just going to say it normally.'

'Bah,' sulked Friday – but Mrs Lovely was determined to tell her tale her own way.

'It was like this,' she began. 'You know how I'm always after unusual herbs to make my sweets? Well, the best ones grow up on Goblin Mountain. So, early this morning, up I did climb to get at those herbs. But soon a blizzard whipped up. I couldn't see a thing – and then, suddenly, I found myself under attack from creatures unknown! They bit and scratched and I thought I was doomed, but somehow I fought my way loose and escaped. After that I don't remember anything and now here I am safe and sound, hooray.'

'What do you thinks them creatures was?' asked Polly.

'I'm not sure,' said Mrs Lovely. 'That's why they were creatures unknown. But like I say, it happened on Goblin Mountain, just outside the Goblin Cave, where the Goblin River runs swift and blue.'

'Hmm,' said Friday thoughtfully, twirling his famous imaginary detective's moustache . . . '*Goblin* Mountain . . . *Goblin* Cave . . . Hmm . . . Goblins . . . Goblins . . . It all points to one thing. Mrs Lovely,' he announced triumphantly, 'it was badgers who attacked you. A gang of wild badgers driven mad by the cold winter and too much sugar!'

'We'll gets 'em!' cried Polly, sticking her head out of the window towards Goblin Mountain. '**Oi! Badgers!**' she shouted, just in case they could hear over long distances like whales or telephones. '**You gone too far this time, you stripy rascals! We gonna come an' sort you out!**'

During all this Alan Taylor had been sitting in an ashtray on the bedside table, listening carefully. And now it was his turn to speak.

For he knew all about the natural world, and that was why he was the headmaster of Saint Pterodactyl's School For The Poor.

'I don't think it was badgers,' he said. 'You see, badgers mainly come out at night and Mrs Lovely was attacked by day. Also, badgers tend to attack small mammals such as stoats, voles and marmots (a type of large ground squirrel). They hardly ever attack Mrs Lovely. You know what I think it was?'

'Badgers?' asked Friday, who hadn't really been listening properly.

'No,' said Alan Taylor, 'I think it was goblins.'

'Goblins?!' whispered Polly in fright.

'Goblins?!' moaned Mrs Lovely fearfully.

'Goblins,' nodded Alan Taylor gravely, and the moon slid out from behind a cloud and its light spilled into the room like a long skeletal finger. And from up high on Goblin Mountain, they seemed to hear horrible laughter, it was probably just their imagination but it gave 'em goosebumps all the same.

Chapter 3

In the Court of the Goblin King

So let us go now, far, far from the room at the tavern where our heroes sit covered in goosebumps. Far, far from the high street, where Martin Launderette is working on a

VERY SECRET INVENTION which probably won't get explained until a bit later. Far, far from the woods on the edge of town, where Friday's secret cottage lies hidden. Far, far from Lamonic Bibber and away we go, over the frozen fields and streams, until we come to a place where the snow falls like Frankenstein's dandruff and the wind howls like Dracula stubbing his big toe on a coffee table. Where the way is hard and steep and twisty, and where no sunlight ever seems to fall – Goblin Mountain!

Wippy →

Captain Ankles ↘

Up, up the cold, bare mountainside
we go, almost to the very top,
until we come to a horrible
gaping hole, all ragged and
torn from the rock. And there is a
terrible din coming from that hole,
like nothing ever heard before.
For 'tis Goblin Cave,
and 'tis ram packed full of
. . . GOBLINS!

Dweezil ↗

Oink Balloon ↘

Funk-Whistle ↗

Big Steve

Big ones, weeny ones, sort of
in-betweeny ones. Goblins!
Bald ones, hairy ones, dirty great big
scary ones. Goblins!
Giant ones, tiny ones, nasty little
spiny ones. Goblins!
Stinky ones, clean ones, not really,
they were all stinky.

GOBLINS!

Livermonk

Yak Triangle

Hey, it's Livermonk again!

Yes, wherever you looked, it was tails and spikes and fins and fur and extra arms and knobbly knees and all sorts. One of the goblins even had two heads, and sat there constantly arguing with himself, no he didn't, yes he did, no he didn't.

Oh, and talk about badly behaved! Those goblins were always up to mischief – scratching and

Yak Triangle having a 'friendly word' with another goblin

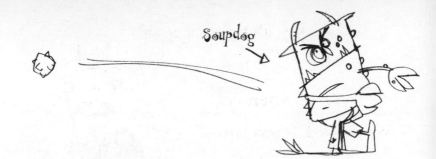

Soupdog

biting, hanging from the ceiling and gobbing on the ones below, cheating at Monopoly, you name it. The only time they ever shut up was when the Goblin King arrived to give his commands.

Mr Boomerang

André Crabtree

Jingles

No one even knows this one's name

And there he sat, right in the middle of all that chaos, sprawled on a great throne made from a rusty dentist's chair he'd found on the mountainside one afternoon. His eyes were red and bloodshot, and his long cruel fingers dripped with silver rings he'd stolen off old-age pensioners. And in his big red beard sat a dark green emerald, gleaming nastily. My word, those goblins loved that big fat jewel! 'SHINY FING!' they'd cry whenever it caught the light. 'SHINY

FING! SHINY FING! SHINY FINNNNG!' All their shouting drove the Goblin King crazy, but he had to put up with it. It was just part of the job.

At the King's side stood his partner in dirt, a shady character known only as Burger Wizard the Third. He wore a robe made from an old sack which said **LOW QUALITY PORK CHOPS**, and he was smoking a pipe full of mud.

'Fancy a little puff, me old Goblin King?' coughed the Burger Wizard, brandishing the pipe.

'It's really nice,' he lied through another cough.

'Get lost, phlegmy,' replied the Goblin King. 'Where's me supper? I'm starvin' me face off here!'

'No problem,' said the Burger Wizard, or B.W. for short. He reached into his filthy robe and pulled out a bunch of steaming chicken entrails.

'Delicious,' growled the Goblin King, swallowing them down whole. 'Now. I got important Kingy stuff to do.

'Mighty Goblin Army!' he commanded. 'Tell

me your news, or I'll give you a Chinese burn!'

At this the Captain of the Goblin Army ran forward, his Lieutenant at his side.

'News goooood,' Captain Ankles reported. 'We attacked oldd womman an' duffed her upp!'

'Who cares about some stupid old woman?' roared the Goblin King. 'What I wants to know is how me evil plan's comin' along! You built that tunnel yet?'

'Nearly finnished!' squealed the Lieutenant,

whose name was Oink Balloon. 'One more day diggging, thenn we finally there!'

'That's more like it,' snorted the Goblin King. 'Now for a nice long snooze.' He closed his eyes and put his feet up –

'SHINY FING! SHINY FINNNNG!' screamed the goblins, pointing at the emerald in his beard and jumping up and down like carrot cakes.

'Shabba me whiskers,' scowled the King.

'These creatures is noisy. Whoever thought leadin' a Goblin Army would be such a bother?'

Chapter 4

You're A Bad Man, Mr Launderette!

The next morning dawned cold and clear in Lamonic Bibber. Martin Launderette was up early to work on his **VERY SECRET INVENTION** when Jonathan Ripples happened to stroll by. He was eating a very large sandwich filled with smaller sandwiches.

Now, Jonathan Ripples might have been fat – in fact, he definitely was – but he wasn't stupid.

'Ho, Martin, what's all this?' he asked, pointing towards the strange device. There were tubes and pipes coming off it and a big motor attached to the back and a wide round hole in the front.

'It's just a washing machine,' said Martin Launderette innocently. 'I do run a launderette, you know.'

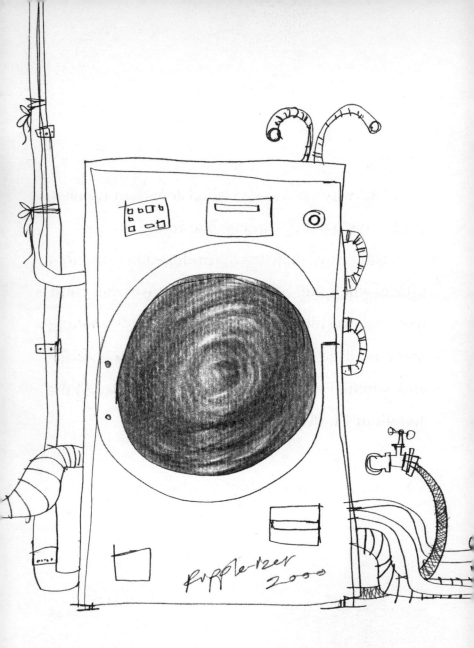

'But why's it so big?' asked Jonathan Ripples, poking his head in through the round door.

Oh, how Martin Launderette chuckled inside when he heard this. Because the truth was, he wasn't just building any old washing machine. He was building the *Ripple-izer 2000* and when it was ready he was going to shove Jonathan Ripples inside and start it up.

He always acts so high and mighty! thought Martin. *Well, the Ripple-izer 2000 will rinse the smile off his fat face once and for all! It won't kill him or anything, because this is a children's book. But it will teach that flabberwhopper a lesson, all right!*

'You're not up to shenanigans, are you?' said Jonathan Ripples, who knew the launderette owner only too well.

'Who, me?' protested Martin Launderette.

'Gosh, no. I'm simply building a really big washing machine, that's all. One that you could fit into – but that's just a complete coincidence.'

'Hmm,' said Jonathan Ripples suspiciously, and off he waddled in all his glorious bulk.

Chapter 5
The Meeting at the Stone Table

Meanwhile, over at the Stone Table on the other side of town, there was serious business taking place. Now, the Stone Table was a mysterious and powerful object of Ancient Times, and it stood in a field of long grass, surrounded by questions and long grass.

How old was it?

Who had built it?

What had it been used for, so long ago?

No one knew the answers, but the best guess came from a famous scientist called Crunchy.

'I have done careful scientific experiments with a ruler,' declared Crunchy, 'and I estimate that this Stone Table is over TWENTY YEARS OLD. And I estimate it was built by PEOPLE. And

I estimate it was originally used AS A TABLE. Now I am off to mess around in pyramids and dig up a mummy because that is what scientists do.'

███

And now, sitting around the Stone Table in the thin December sunshine were Friday, Alan Taylor and Polly, all looking very solemn indeed.

'Good friends,' began Friday. 'I have

gathered you here this winter's morn because Father Christmas has been kidnapped by an evil sparrow who wants all the presents for himself! And it is up to us to come to his rescue –'

'Friday,' sighed Polly. 'That's just that film we watched last week, *A Very Sparrowy Christmas*, remember?'

'Not really,' said Friday truthfully. 'So why *have* I gathered you here this winter's morn?'

'Because Mrs Lovely got attacked on Goblin

Mountain,' said Alan Taylor. 'Remember?'

'Not really,' said Friday truthfully. 'Now listen, friends. Last night a wise dream came to me and a strange voice spoke unto me and it said:

"Hello, Friday. How are you? I like your hat. Oh, by the way, you must go on a brave quest and sort out those goblins before things get worse."

'The voice said I must go up Goblin Mountain,' continued Friday. 'And I must go armed only with pure thoughts, an honest tongue and a brave heart. Plus a sword in case all that stuff doesn't work. And so, friends, I depart at noon. But I will need to pick one other brave traveller to accompany me on my quest.'

'Oh, pick me, pick me, please!!' cried Polly.

'Sorry,' said Friday, shaking his head in a little gesture he'd invented to mean 'no'.

(Everyone in Lamonic Bibber used his ingenious system – why not try it yourself?)

'I have decided to take Yellowbeard instead,' said Friday. And he pointed to a thickset dwarf with a bushy black beard who sat by his side, dressed in chain mail and carrying a battleaxe. Until that moment Polly hadn't noticed him there.

'Yellowbeard?' protested Polly. 'But Friday, we're a team, you an' me! Together we're the very best at adventures an' suchlike!'

'Sorry,' said Friday. 'But Yellowbeard the dwarf it is. And he's my new best friend, by the way.'

Well, just then Alan Taylor gave a little giggle and suddenly Polly realised what was going on.

Hold on, she thought. *This looks like one of Friday's 'mazin' jokes!*

She took a closer look and saw that Yellowbeard was just made out of cardboard. Friday had been up most of the night cutting him out and colouring him in with felt tips.

'Oh, Frides!' laughed Polly, pushing Yellowbeard over into the snow. 'You an' your 'mazin' jokes!'

'THE TRUTH IS A LEMON MERINGUE!' laughed Friday affectionately. 'Of course you're coming with me, Polly!'

'And I will stay and look after Mrs Lovely,' proclaimed Alan Taylor. 'I will teach her about the natural world with my collection of wildlife documentaries. I've got a brilliant one about leopards. They are fascinating creatures, and the spots on their fur are known as "spots".'

'It is well said, sir,' remarked Friday, taking out his tuba. 'Now let us all sing a song to bring this great meeting at the Stone Table to an end. I love songs.'

'Sorry,' said Alan Taylor, looking at his tiny

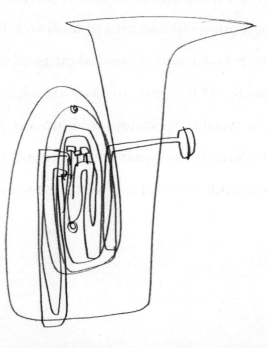

chocolate wristwatch. 'No time for singing –
we've got to get you two ready.'

And the meeting was done.

The rest of the morning was spent preparing for
the quest. Alan Taylor scampered off to buy pies,
for he knew the most about baked goods, being
one himself. Polly ran to buy thick cloaks,
because it would be bitter cold up on Goblin
Mountain. And Friday played a computer game
down the arcade and got a really high score.

Eventually noon came round, as noon always does. Good old noon, it never lets you down. And it was time for the quest to begin.

'Farewell, good travellers,' said Alan Taylor, as Polly hugged him goodbye.

'Farewell, my crumbly friend,' said Friday, stooping to tickle the little fellow under the chin. And, having said their goodbyes, the courageous pair turned on their heels and started off down the long and winding road that would take them to Goblin Mountain.

It had started to snow once more, soft white flakes that fell from the sky like angels' tears. Soon the travellers were just dots in the distance and eventually Alan Taylor could not make them out at all.

'Tis a brave and lonely day, he thought as he stood there, shivering in the icy wind. *Will I ever see those two again?*

Then he ate his chocolate wristwatch. It sort of spoilt the moment but he'd missed breakfast.

Chapter 6
The Great Gifts

I t was coming on dark by the time Polly and Friday reached the foot of Goblin Mountain. The craggy rock loomed over them forbiddingly in the dismal gloom, all twisted like ~~one of those crazy curly twirly funtime drinking straws you sometimes get. They're hilarious~~! an old witch's finger.

'Polly,' said Friday, ruffling Polly's hair affectionately with a hair-ruffling machine set to the 'affectionate' setting. 'Are you absolutely four hundred per cent sure you want to do this?'

But before Polly could answer, the wind howled louder than ever, and up blew a great blanket of snow, turning the world completely white so she couldn't see a thing.

'Friday!' yelled Polly in the sudden emptiness. 'What's a-happenin'?'

'I don't knooooooow!' came Friday's reply – but he sounded a very long way off and in between all that wind and snow, Polly didn't know which way was which. And now she seemed to hear peculiar noises – wolves a-howling, haunting voices from the past, doorbells ringing in outer space, the sound of a milkmaid sitting on a watermelon . . .

'Meep,' whimpered Polly in a small voice. 'It's all crazy an' scary, like them late night films on TV what isn't for children's eyes!'

But then the unsettling noises were replaced by another sound, faint at first but growing louder. It was the merry tinkle of a music box, and as it grew in strength the blanket of snow cleared clean away. With some surprise, Polly saw she was still standing at the foot of the mountain, although for some reason Friday was halfway up a fir tree.

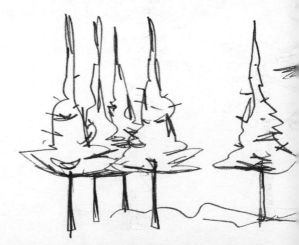

And now the sound of the music box seemed to be everywhere as a small boy came walking towards them through the snow. And just seeing that boy filled the travellers with warmth, for it was none other than the Spirit of the Rainbow.

'Child,' he greeted Polly, though he was no older than she. 'For weeks I have lain awake thinking about your brave journey.'

'But we only thought of settin' off this very mornin',' said Polly in wonder.

'I see many things,' came the boy's amazing reply. 'Past and future, it does not matter which, for I see it all.'

'Spirit of the Rainbow,' said Friday, climbing down from the fir tree. 'YOU were the voice in my dream, telling me to come on this quest! You were, weren't you, you little scamp!'

'Old man, I've no idea what you're on about,' answered the lad. 'But you will soon face great troubles, so I have come to help you on your way.'

And then the Spirit of the Rainbow turned his face to the sky and spoke a few strange words, words from long ago before the World began.

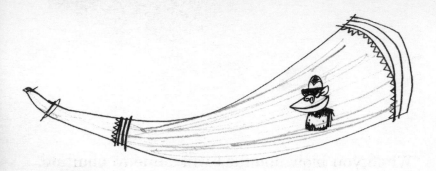

And when he turned back a moment later, he was bearing Great Gifts in his honest hands.

'Here,' he said. And very solemnly he presented Friday with a fabulous horn. It shimmered with all the colours of the Universe, and it had a cool picture of a monkey wearing sunglasses on the side.

'Behold! The legendary Horn of Q'zaal Q'zaal, forged thousands of years ago by the High Otter Priests of Bastos,' said the boy.

'When you blow upon it I will come to your aid. But be warned – you may use it only once. After that it is powerless forever.'

Then the boy turned to Polly and handed her his second gift. It was a fruit chew.

'Behold!' said the boy, 'the Fruit Chew of Babylon. It might not look as good as the Horn of Q'zaal Q'zaal,' he admitted. 'But a time may come when you learn of its true greatness.'

'Thank you,' said Polly. 'But, please – won't you come with us an' help us out?'

'I wish I could,' sighed the Spirit of the Rainbow. 'But long ago before the World began, I made a deal with Robert, the Creator of All Things. And the deal is that I can only help out every now and then. Besides, I have to revise for my maths exam or my Mum will kill me.'

'Spirit!' called a voice from down the way. 'You get inside right now an' learn yer fractions!'

'See?' said the Spirit of the Rainbow. And off he ran.

'I bet it WAS him in my dream,' said Friday, watching him go. 'That's just the sort of thing he'd get up to.'

🎁 🎁 🎁

So, armed with their Great Gifts, the travellers continued on their way feeling far more courageous than before. But their courage would have turned to porridge and been eaten by the

Bears of Doubt if they'd known who was watching them. For high up in his cave, the Goblin King was observing the travellers' every move.

Chapter 7
The Three Impossible Challenges

'BLEM!' yelled the Goblin King furiously as he peered into a golden telescope he'd 'borrowed' from a department store. 'It's them meddlers! Comin' up the mountain to meddle with me tunnel-diggin' plans, no doubt!'

'Don't fret, me old shoelace,' coughed the Burger Wizard, choking on a pipe full of horse fat. 'They'll never make it past the Three Impossible Challenges.'

'Phew,' said the Goblin King. 'I'd forgotten about them blurpin' challenges what all travellers climbing Goblin Mountain have to face. Oho,' he cried, turning back to the telescope, 'here comes the first challenge now!'

'This is gonna be really funty!' snickered B.W.

(You see, that was how the Burger Wizard pronounced the word 'funny'.)

CHALLENGE ONE ~ THE TROLL

At that precise moment down on the mountainside the earth shook and trembled, and a dirty great troll stepped out from behind a boulder. He had greasy hair because he only bought cheap shampoo, and like all proper trolls he carried a knobbly wooden club with a nail through it. Oh, he was a fearsome sight. As tall as three men he was, and he went to the gym every week to keep his muscles strong for crushing travellers, and also to impress the girl trolls. Polly hid behind Friday, and Friday hid behind an atom but it was no good – the troll spotted them anyway.

'RIGHT,' he shouted in a great booming voice. 'SHUT UP AND DON'T MOVE!' He took a roll of parchment from his nostril and began to read:

To Whom I Am About To Eat:

You have stepped on to my patch of the mountain like the fools you are. And now you must face my challenge, you idiots. And it is a mighty challenge indeed! No one has ever succeeded in beating me at this challenge, not in hundreds of years. And the challenge is this: You cannot get past me unless you guess my name. And you will **NEVER** guess my name. And when you have **FAILED** to guess my name, I will **CRUSH YOUR BONES UP** and **EAT** you. And **THAT** is my challenge.

Yours sincerely

Arthur the Troll

'This looks like trouble,' Friday gulped. 'Shall we blow the Horn of Q'zaal Q'zaal?'

'Nah, we only gets one go at that,' said Polly. 'I reckon we can handle this one.'

Bravely she stepped forward.

'Your name is Arthur the Troll,' said Polly. 'An' don't lie cos I know it is! Now yangle off, hairy!'

'Lucky guess,' muttered Arthur the Troll as he yangled off. 'I'm going to the gym.'

'NO WAY!' shouted the Goblin King in disbelief. 'Somehow them meddlers got past the troll!'

'Don't you worry,' laughed B.W. 'It's the witch next! That'll muck 'em up!'

CHALLENGE TWO ~ THE WITCH

Down on the mountain a secret door in a rock opened with a scary creaking sound and a witch came out, hobbling along with her little bent back and leaning on a cane.

'I'm gonna do spells on you!' she cackled. 'Yes, that's right – spells! I'm gonna muck you up!'

'Did you hear that?' said Friday in fright. 'Spells!'

'Quick!' said Polly. 'Blow the Horn of Q'zaal – hold on a moment! She's not gettin' nowhere near us!'

It was true. The witch was moving along at about one centimetre a minute. As the travellers watched, she was overtaken by a dead snail.

'When I get near enough I'm gonna do spells!' called the witch, brandishing her cane. 'Then you'll be sorry! Spells!'

Friday and Polly looked at each other.

'Shall we escape now or later?' said Friday.

'Later,' said Polly. 'After supper.'

So Friday fetched some sticks to start a fire, and Polly took out the pies and some apples, and they made a fine meal. And all the while the witch inched along, occasionally calling out her threats.

After they had eaten, the travellers sat and talked awhile. Then they played a few games of backgammon, and after that they did a 10,000 piece jigsaw puzzle. Altogether it was a very jolly time but eventually Friday stood up.

'Well, we'd better hurry off or the witch will catch us in a few hours,' he said. So up Polly got and together they continued on their way.

'Just you wait 'til I'm close enough to do my spells!' the witch called after them, shaking her fist very slowly. Moss was growing on her shoes. 'Then you'll be sorry!'

'UNBELIEVABLE!' screamed the Goblin King, staring into the telescope. 'Somehow them meddlers beat the witch an' all!'

'True,' admitted B.W. 'But they'll never survive the final challenge.'

'What, that thing that looks like a gherkin?' sneered the Goblin King. 'Come off it, he's the easiest one of the lot.'

CHALLENGE THREE ~ THAT THING THAT LOOKS LIKE A GHERKIN

Down on the mountain, the thing that looked like a gherkin rolled menacingly towards the travellers. Friday stepped on it with his boot and they continued on their way.

🥒 🥒 🥒

'FRIMP!' shouted the Goblin King. 'If you ask me, them Impossible Challenges is a load of old toilet. Hoi! Captain Ankles!' he called – and instantly the Goblin Captain appeared, accompanied by his faithful Lieutenant, Oink Balloon.

'Now, listen, Ankles,' said the Goblin King. 'I wants you to go an' capture some meddlers for me. It's a big important job, right, so take yer best soldiers with you. Take Wippy, Livermonk,

Big Steve, Funk-Whistle, Soupdog, Jingles and Yak Triangle. An' don't you let me down, Ankles, or I'll introduce you to me bashin' fist!'

Once he'd dealt with that, the Goblin King turned to more important matters.

'Oi, Burger Wizard, where's me supper?' he demanded.

'Right here, me old balaclava,' laughed B.W., holding up a plate of greenish meat and thistles.

And there in the cave the two ruffians dined

on their slops like common swine, while all around the goblins shrieked and hooted and roared.

'Ha ha ha!' laughed the Goblin King through a mouthful of pig's bladder. 'This is the life!'

Chapter 8
Night on Goblin Mountain

As night fell, the travellers were making camp. Polly lit a fire and Friday found a wild rabbit to cook, which was lucky because he was too tired to cook for himself. The rabbit whipped up some omelettes while the travellers gazed out over the mountainside into the vast, starry night.

Far below, the lights of Lamonic Bibber twinkled welcomingly. The houses looked warm and inviting, and Polly imagined she could hear the happy laughter of children coming from within. In the middle of town a plume of blue smoke was just visible. It was coming from Martin Launderette's **VERY SECRET INVENTION**, the *Ripple-izer 2000*.

Gazing over the scene, Polly felt tears well up in her eyes, not just because the rabbit was peeling an onion, but because she realised how much she loved Lamonic Bibber, every last bit of it.

'I loves that town,' she said fiercely, and her heart swelled with pride as she spoke. 'It's the best place in the world an' I don't never wants to live nowhere else, that's all I got to say on the subject, the end.'

'Well said, Polly,' nodded Friday. He himself felt a little homesick for his secret cottage in the woods and a nice Sunday roast and sitting on Mrs Lovely's lap, eating yogurts. 'Tell you what,' he said, taking out his grand piano. 'This is the perfect moment for a song. I've a new one I've been working on. It's called "Me And Uncle Radish".

ME AND UNCLE RADISH

Well, me and Uncle Radish
We go everywhere together –'

'Shh,' whispered Polly urgently, putting out the fire with a mug of water. 'I think I done heard somethin' a-creepin' in the bushes.'

Polly and Friday huddled together, trembling in the darkness. After a minute the rabbit joined them, twitching its whiskers like a total wurly. And now they could all hear the noises – strange hisses and creaks and moans. And then they heard a twig snap. Then another snapped – and then another.

And then the moon it did come out from behind a cloud, and in its silvery light the travellers saw the game was up. For they were completely surrounded by goblins, standing there snapping twigs in their bumpy old hands.

'GETT THEMM!' commanded Captain Ankles and at this the goblins advanced, eyes wide and claws glinting wickedly.

'The poor rabbit!' cried Polly. 'This isn't no place for you, little one,' she said, scooping it up in her arms and carrying it to a safe place underneath a bush. You see, that was just the sort of girl Polly was – she always looked out for people smaller than herself, especially if they were rabbits.

'Right,' said Friday. 'Now leave the rest to me!' And he reached for his broadsword, the legendary LORD CHAMPION. It was made from the strongest steel known to man and it shone like a Flaming Star of Justice and nothing could defeat it in battle and it was lying on Friday's sofa in his secret cottage next to an empty yogurt pot.

'Brummigans!' cursed Friday. 'Forgot the broadsword.' But then he had an idea.

'Get back, you monsters!' he warned, doing a mime as if he was holding a mighty sword after all. 'Or taste the blade of my legendary invisible broadsword, TRANSPARENT-O, which has slain many, many goblins and trolls. And an elk.'

The goblins hissed and started to back off. But not Captain Ankles. He wasn't fooled for a moment.

'Invisiball sword not reall!' he said. 'Old bloke jusst pretennding! Look, he jusst miming!'

And then the travellers were done for. The goblins advanced again and this time there was no stopping them.

They threw Polly and Friday into a great big sack and tied it up with dirty magic string you can't escape from unless you're Harry Potter. Then they lifted the sack above their gruesome heads and back up the mountain they started, hooting and shouting to wake the dead.

From beneath the bush, the little rabbit watched the whole terrible scene. *I will never forget that brave girl who carried me to safety*, its bright green eyes seemed to say. *Well, I might. But I'll try really hard not to.*

👁 👁 👁

'Polly,' whispered Friday hopefully as they were bumped and bundled along in the sack. 'Are you Harry Potter?'

'No,' said Polly. 'I'm Polly.'

'That's what I thought,' said Friday gloomily.

'Can you reach the Horn?' said Polly. 'I thinks this might be a good time to summon the Spirit of the Rainbow.'

But try as he might, Friday couldn't reach it, and with their last hope gone, the prisoners fell silent, each fearing the worst. And on the goblins marched. On and on and on, all night long they marched. Until, by the time they finally reached Goblin Cave, a grey dawn was breaking over the mountain and the crows cawed mournfully in the bare trees.

'Helllo! Gobbblin King! We catched the meddlers!' Captain Ankles called out.

'Shut up!' came a familiar voice. 'I'm tryin' to watch "Bag of Sticks"!'

There's somethin' familiar 'bout that familiar voice, thought Polly, but in all the commotion as she and Friday were carried through the cave, she couldn't work out what.

'HALT!' she heard Captain Ankles say, and then Oink Balloon ripped open the sack with his claws, and the travellers were face to face with the Goblin King himself.

'You flippin' hasslers,' spat the Goblin King, coming so close that Polly could smell his meaty old breath. 'Don't you know I'm the best cos I'm so powerful an' handsome?' And suddenly, Polly realised the dreadful truth.

Fry me in vegetable oil an' call me a giant bag of crisps! she thought to herself. *The Goblin King is Mr Gum! Oh, and there's Billy William, he's probbly callin' himself the Burger Wizard or somethin', I 'spect.'*

Chapter 9

Polly and Friday in the Cave

'Well, well, well,' said Mr Gum. The emerald in his beard glinted and shone as if somehow laughing at them, and the goblins chanted 'SHINY FING! SHINY FING! SHINY FING!' until Polly felt she was in a nightmare – but

she knew nightmares didn't smell so bad, so it must be real.

'Here am I,' spat Mr Gum, 'mindin' me own business an' just bein' a flippin' Goblin King like nature intended – an' you two have to come an' spoil all me good work!'

'You calls duffin' up Mrs Lovely "good work"?' shot back Polly. 'Mr Gum, you make me as sick as an alligator. Hey, Friday!' she yelled.

'Blow that horn – an' make it funky!'

Friday snatched up the Horn of Q'zaal Q'zaal and brought it to his lips.

'Oh, Spirit of the Rainbow, come to us now,' he pleaded.

And on that horn he did blow.

MMMAAAAAARI

A long, marmping note flew out into the cave. It went bouncing off the walls, bashed Captain Ankles in the belly and flew out over the mountainside. And down in Lamonic Bibber the townsfolk awoke and their hearts were filled with joy to hear that gorgeous noise. The birds sang, the sun shone and a dead flower on Old Granny's windowsill came back to life and started growing golden pears.

'Right,' said Friday when the last strains of the glorious note had faded. 'Any second now, you're going to be absolutely Rainbowed like you've never been Rainbowed before.'

Everyone waited.

Friday checked his watch.

Mr Gum picked his nose.

Someone sneezed.

'Yup,' said Friday, a little less confidently this time. 'He'll be here any . . . second . . . now. Hey!' he shouted helpfully to the Spirit of the Rainbow, in case he had taken a wrong turn. 'We're over here! In a cave!'

'OK,' said Mr Gum eventually. 'He's obviously not turnin' up. I 'spect he's scared cos he knows I'm simply too powerful, an' I'm excellent at punchin'. So let's just get on wiv things! Mighty Goblin Army!' he cried –

'Excuse me,' said Friday. 'Are you about to tell the goblins your plan?'

'Yeah,' said Mr Gum. 'So what?'

'Well, would you mind doing it as a song?' asked Friday. 'I love songs.'

'You lunatic!' said Mr Gum, shaking his head in disgust. 'Your brain's too small for your head, that's your problem, O'Leary!

'Now, goblins,' he continued. 'Our hour has finally come. Today we starts down that tunnel what we bin buildin', I never told you why, but now I'm a-gonna. That tunnel goes right down through this flabberin' mountain, an' guess where it comes out? Lamonic Bibber!'

At this, the goblins shrieked with joy, Polly gasped in horror and Friday did the splits in amazement.

'So, me little goblin-goblins, the plan is this,' explained Mr Gum. 'We sneaks down that old tunnel, we bursts out – an' we takes everyone by surprise! An' before they knows what's what, it ain't Lamonic Bibber no more. It's Goblin City, an' we can run wild an' drink beer all the livelong day!'

'YEAH!' screamed the goblins. 'Gobbblin Citty! Gobbblin Citty!'

'Sorry but no, Mr Gum!' said Polly. 'I loves that town an' you'll never turn it into no goblin paradise full of litter an' dog mess everywhere!'

'Oh, no? What are you gonna do about it?' laughed Mr Gum. And he stretched out his arms and chanted:

Burger Wizard!
Do that thing!
That thing with the burgers!
Goo goo g'joob!

And suddenly the air was full of hamburgers as Billy William did what he liked doing best – throwing bad meat at good people. Golly, his hands were just a blur as he spun those burgers fast and furious like horrid grey frisbees.

'It's supper time!' he cackled, launching a quarter pounder straight at Polly's knee. 'Enjoy your meal!'

'Oh, Mrs Lovely,' said Friday, as he and Polly backed away from the gristly missiles. 'I know you cannot hear me, but I love you more than a man ever loved a woman. I love you like the sun loves the stars and like swordfishes love swimming through the sea trying to stab things with their sharp faces. I was hoping that one day you'd tell me your first name – but alas, Mrs Lovely, it is not to be. For now I go to my doom and – A A A A A R R R G G G H ! '

Suddenly he was falling, falling, falling through pitch black . . . And Polly was falling, falling, falling with him. Together they fell, fell, fell. That bit wasn't too bad – but then they landed, landed, landed. And it hurt, hurt, hurt.

'OOF!' said Friday as he landed on a hard stone floor. 'YUMK!' he exclaimed as Polly landed on top of him. 'CHURP!' he added, just because he felt like it.

'W-what happened?' asked Polly in confusion, but then Mr Gum's bloodshot eyes appeared far above, glaring down at them.

'You've fallen down the old abandoned well,' grinned Mr Gum. 'I knew that was gonna happen,' he lied. 'It was all part of me ingenious plan, probably.'

'Yeah,' said Billy William, appearing at his side. 'An' now we're goin' down our tunnel with all them goblins, an' soon we'll be runnin' things!'

'Yeah,' agreed Mr Gum. 'An' here's a thing, O'Leary. When we go down that tunnel, we're gonna do a brilliant song, with yodelling an' everythin'. An' you're gonna miss every incredible second of it!'

'Oh, no!' wailed Friday. 'How can this be happening? HOW? It's just not fair!'

'Right,' said Mr Gum, affectionately kicking Billy William as hard as possible in the shins.

'Let's get goin', me old Burger Wizard. We got songs to sing an' tunnels to go down!'

And then they were gone, and Polly and Friday were left alone in the dark.

Chapter 10
The Tunnel Song*

featuring a special burp solo from Livermonk the goblin

GOBLIN KING: *I am the Goblin King*
Listen to me sing
Yodel-odel-odel-odel-ay!

BURGER WIZARD: *And I'm the Burger Wizard*
Listen to me play
Yodel-odel-odel all the day!

WIPPY: My name Wippy!
Yoda! Yoda! Yoda!

GOBLIN KING: Shut up, Wippy!
It's not your flippin' turn!
Yodel-odel-odel-odel ay!

OINK BALLOON: My name Oinky Balloo!
Yogurt! Yogurt! Ay! Ay! Ay!

BURGER WIZARD: Shut up, Oink Balloon!
It's not your turn neither, you stupid moron.
I can't believe you goblins don't know when
to sing an' when not to sing, you're
mucking everythin' up!
Yodel-odel-odel-odel ay!

126

CHORUS: Let's go down the tunnel!
Let's go down the tunnel!
Let's go down the tunnel!
Let's go down the tunnel!

Let's go down the tunnel!
Yes, let's go down the tunnel!
Let's go down the tunnel!
Tunnels are quite good.

GOBLIN KING: Now, Livermonk! Burp solo! Take it away!

LIVERMONK: BURP! BURP! BURP! BURP! BURP!
BURP! BURP! BURP! BURP! BURP!
BURP! BURP! BURP! BURP! BURP!
BURP! BURP! BURP! BURP! BURP!
BURP! BURP! BURP! BURP! BURP!
BURP! BURP! BURP! BURP! BURP!
BURP! BURP! BURP! BURP! BURP!
BURP! BUR–

Dear Readers,

We here at Egmont Books have decided that this song has gone on far too long already. It is in the worst possible taste and we are stopping it RIGHT NOW. We had no idea it would be quite so awful. Sorry, everyone.

Signed

Mr Egmont

Mr Egmont, the Publisher

Mrs Egmont

And his wife, Mrs Egmont*

*Actually just Mr Egmont wearing a dress

And now . . . back to the story.

Chapter 11

Heroes in the Snow

Polly and Friday lay at the bottom of the well, in the darkest darkness they had ever not seen. The goblins were on their smelly way to Lamonic Bibber and there was nothing they could do about it.

'I can't believe I missed the song,' Friday said miserably. 'I bet it was magnificent.'

'I bet you it wasn't,' said Polly. 'Knowing Mr Gum, it was probbly full of mistakes an' burpin' an' what-have-you. Now let's see what's goin' on 'round here an' maybe we can escape.'

Together they scrabbled about in the darkness and soon their hands found something smooth and cold. It was the side of the old well.

'Maybe we can move these bricks,' said Polly

eagerly, and they set to work pulling and pushing at the stonework. But no – those bricks weren't going anywhere. They'd been there for hundreds of years and they fancied being there for hundreds of years more and that was their final word on the matter. After a while Polly collapsed back in the darkness.

'I hates it!' she fumed. 'Mr Gum's just left us here to rot away like snowmen! An' what's more –'

Just then one of the bricks shifted a little. Then out it plopped on to the floor.

'Magic bricks!' said Friday, tapping his nose wisely. 'I thought as much!'

But for once in his life, Friday was wrong. A little face peeked out of the hole where the brick had been.

'Why, it's that rabbit!' gasped Polly.

And yes, it really was. Because that rabbit hadn't forgotten Polly's kindness and somehow it had known she was in trouble. So through the mountain it had burrowed, and those stupid bricks were no match for its powerful digging legs.

Now follow me, the rabbit's bright green eyes seemed to say – and the travellers crawled through the burrow after the long-eared superhero. The passageway twisted and turned until Polly lost all track of time and Friday lost one of his shoes, but eventually they saw moonlight shining up ahead.

Sweet, sweet moonlight! And out they climbed into the cold starry night.

'Thank you, little one,' said Polly, bending down to shake the rabbit's paw.

My work here is done, the rabbit's bright green eyes seemed to say. *Now it is up to you, travellers. Only you can save the day with your bravery and courage. The way is hard, but I have faith in you because I am a rabbit.*

'Wow,' said Friday as the creature bounded

off into the darkness. 'I've never met a rabbit with such talkative eyes.'

'Never mind that,' said Polly. 'We're still ages away from Lamonic Bibber, an' them goblins is easy gonna beat us back there before we can warn the townsfolk!'

It looked totally hopeless, but just then –

'Hark,' said Friday. 'What sound is this, coming our way this blustery night? Why, it almost sounds like – yes, it is – barking!'

'Could it be?' said Polly, hardly daring to believe it was true. 'Could it be?' she repeated, jumping on Friday's shoulders to get a better look. 'YES!' she cried excitedly. 'GOAL! NUMBER 1 HIT RECORD ON THE CHARTS! GOLD MEDAL! EXTRA LIFE! BRAND NEW PENCIL CASE!'

You see, these were all the best things Polly could think of – because rattling through the fields on his huge friendly paws was her old friend, Jake the dog! And a fine, fine dog was he!

There were sleigh bells all over his tail and an enormous Christmas tree stuck to his back,

and right at the top like the star he was sat little Alan Taylor, scanning the fields with his juicy raisin eyes.

'There they are!' the biscuity fellow beamed when he saw the travellers. And as Jake came belting towards them, Polly laughed to see who was steering him, for it was a little boy no older than she.

'Spirit of the Rainbow!' she laughed in pure joy. 'Is it really you?'

'Of course,' replied the lad as Jake pulled up and began licking Polly's eyebrows.

'I promised to come to your aid when the Horn of Q'zaal Q'zaal was blown – and here I am.'

'Thank you, sir,' said Friday graciously. 'But there is one thing I have to ask. Couldn't you have come a bit sooner?'

'Old man,' explained the boy. 'When you blew that horn I was in Newcastle, staying over at my cousin's. I had to catch the train, and it was delayed for ages – and then the taxi from the station broke down, so I had to walk the last two miles on foot. And then I had to – what?' he asked, noticing Friday's surprise. 'You didn't think I would just *magically appear* when you blew the horn, did you? Oh!' laughed the boy as the travellers climbed aboard Jake's festive back. 'The very idea! How you humans do amuse me!'

And then they were all laughing together for the idea of someone just *magically appearing* was simply ridiculous! But now there was no time to lose.

'Mush!' cried the Spirit of the Rainbow, which is something you say to dogs to get them to run really fast through snow, no one knows why. And – **WOOF-PZAAANG!** – Jake took off like a hairy bullet called Jake and there they were, racing back to Lamonic Bibber in the moonlight.

'Alan Taylor,' said Friday as they rode. 'How is my darling wife, Mrs Lovely?'

'Fine, thanks,' chuckled Mrs Lovely, popping her head out from inside the Christmas tree where she'd been hiding for a surprise. 'I'm completely better, tra-la-la-la-la!'

'THE TRUTH IS A LEMON MERINGUE!' shouted Friday happily. Mrs Lovely jumped into his arms, and everyone pretended not to look while they done a bit of kissing and that.

♡ ♡ ♡

The rest of that night passed in a hazy crazy daze, with Jake woofing and yuffling endlessly through the white powdery snow. It was all down to that big bark-machine now, and he ran like no dog has ever run before or since! Actually, one dog has run like that before. His name was Mop Mop and it happened in Denmark in 1974. Mop Mop was chasing a florist through the streets of Copenhagen –

'Who cares about Mop Mop?' cried Polly. 'Come on, Jakey! RUN!'

And so over the frozen fields big Jake ran, hardly even slipping on the icy bits. Through snowdrifts great and small, bounding over walls, he leapt a country stile and ran for miles and miles, while night time turned to day, he ran a long long way, in the jingle jangle morning he went slobbing along.

But is he a-slobbin' along fast enough, that's what I does want to know! thought Polly anxiously.

'Have faith, child,' the Spirit of the Rainbow reassured her, as if he could read her brains. 'And if you can't have faith, have a fruit chew.'

'Hey, that reminds me,' said Polly, fishing out the Fruit Chew of Babylon from her skirt pocket. 'I still gots this Great Gift what you gave me.'

'Patience, child,' said the Spirit of the Rainbow. 'The Fruit Chew of Babylon is powerful but it must be used at just the right moment. For as it is written in the stars, in special space-ink:

**The Fruit Chew Of Babylon
Will Sort Out
The Truth Of It All**

'Whatever can that mean?' wondered Polly – but the Spirit of the Rainbow would say no more. And on they rode in silence, racing desperately against time.

❖ ❖ ❖

Overhead, morning was breaking as Jake rounded one last corner and a familiar sight met Polly's eyes.

'Boaster's Hill!' she exclaimed happily. 'We're back home where we belongs!'

But her happiness didn't last long, because something strange was happening at the bottom of the hill. As the heroes watched, a huge load of soil went flying everywhere. And then, in the blink of a tramp's eye, the goblins burst out from the hillside, spitting and dropping litter all over the place and designing cheap blocks of flats made of concrete. They had only been in Lamonic Bibber for about three seconds but already it was starting to look like Goblin City.

Chapter 12
The Fruit Chew of Babylon

'I am the Head Beekeeper!' yelled Mr Gum as he emerged from the tunnel. (This was just his way of saying 'I am the best!' for Mr Gum admired beekeepers tremendously. And why? Because beekeepers are in charge of bees, and can command them to sting anyone they fancy.)

'Ha, ha, me old stilton! You know what's really gonna be funty?' said Billy William, laughing like a pair of scissors. 'When this here Goblin Army attacks the sleepin' townsfolk!'

'Yeah,' agreed Mr Gum, chuckling as Yak Triangle pushed a bench into the duck pond. 'Cos who knows we're comin'? No one! An' that's what a surprise attack's all about!'

'Wrong!' said a pure clear voice from above, and the villains looked up in amazement to see

the heroes a-standing on the hillside, the sun
gleaming behind them to prove they were
definitely the goodies.

'*This* is what a surprise attack's all about!'
said the Spirit of the Rainbow.

'MEDDLERS!' shouted Mr Gum in fury.

Burger Wizard!
Do that thing!
That thing with the burgers!
Goo goo g'j–

But even before Billy could reach for his first missile, Jake was upon him, knocking him flat to the icy ground. Billy's appalling hamburgers spilled out harmlessly on the ground and the Spirit of the

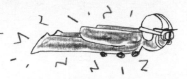

Rainbow swept them away with a broom made by a company called Forces of Good, Limited.

'YEAH!' shouted Polly in triumph. 'Take that, Billy, you unholy lobster!'

'Mr Gum's getting away!' warned Friday.

'I don't think so,' chirruped Mrs Lovely, and she picked up Alan Taylor and swung him through the air towards that so-called Goblin King.

'MAXIMUM GINGERBREAD STRENGTH!' shouted the little biscuit,

even though this didn't really mean anything. He landed in Mr Gum's disgraceful beard and gave a mighty kick at the emerald, sending it flying up into the air. Slowly, slowly it flew, turning lazily in the early morning sunlight, and dozens of little round goblin eyes watched it go. Without thinking, Polly reached out her hand and caught it. And dozens of little round goblin eyes turned in her direction.

'Me emerald!' moaned Mr Gum. 'Me lovely emerald what's rightfully mine, an' what I definitely didn't steal off a rich lady in London last year!'

'SHINY FING!' the goblins cried eagerly. 'SHINY FINNNNG!'

'Uh oh,' said Polly.

'Run, child!' urged the Spirit of the Rainbow.

'Where to?' squeaked Polly.

'Just run,' replied the lad calmly. 'And have faith. When the time is right you will know what to do.'

Well, all Polly knew was that a lot of scary goblins were coming after her, babbling 'SHINY FING!' So she turned tail and off she scooted.

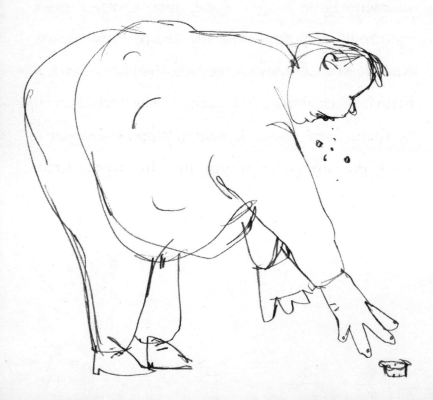

At that exact same moment, there was a knock at
Jonathan Ripples' front door. He went to answer it
and was astonished to find there was nobody there.

'That's strange,' he frowned, but then –

'Ooh!' he remarked. 'What's this?'

He bent down to take a closer look. It was a mince pie, lying innocently on the doorstep. A moment later it was gone, just another poor victim of Jonathan Ripples' unstoppable jaws. But then those jaws spotted another mince pie, a little further along. In fact, there was a whole trail of them. And soon Jonathan Ripples was on a wild pie chase, scoffing up the tasty little scallywags without a thought of where they might be taking him.

'It's like that dream I once had as a boy,' he exclaimed happily as he munched. 'The one about the pies.'

From behind the *Ripple-izer 2000*, Martin Launderette watched his plan unfolding.

'Come on, come on,' he mumbled excitedly. He'd hardly slept for days, his hair was all messed up and he was coated in engine oil and non-biological washing powder.

'I'll show that fatty-come-lately who's the boss once and for all!' he gibbered insanely. 'Come ON!'

Now Jonathan Ripples was three pies away.

Now two.

And now he spied the very last pie. It was the biggest one of all and it was perched right in the doorway of the washing machine.

As if in a trance, Jonathan Ripples waddled forward . . .

He reached for the pie . . .

And Martin Launderette crept up behind him, ready to Ripple-ize . . .

But just then Polly came rushing around the corner, the Goblin Army snapping at her heels.

'I – can't – goes – on – no – more,' she panted. But then she saw the washing machine and for some reason she remembered the words that were written in the stars:

The Fruit Chew Of Babylon
Will Sort Out
The Truth Of It All

And suddenly Polly knew exactly what she had to do. With the last of her strength she raced for the washing machine, shoved Jonathan Ripples aside and chucked the emerald in through the round doorway.

Well, those goblins didn't think twice.

They just piled straight in after it, desperate to get their grabby hands on the shiny green jewel.

'Quick, Mr Ripples, sir! Shut the door!' cried Polly. 'It's too heavy for me, I'm only nine!'

Brave, greedy Jonathan Ripples slammed the door shut and Polly started up the machine. Then she took the legendary Fruit Chew of Babylon from her skirt pocket and popped it into the powder hatch. There wasn't even time to unwrap it.

'I hopes I done it right,' she prayed . . . And two seconds later –

KA-BLLLL UUUURRR MMM-O!

The machine rattled up and down like a baby shaking a wasps' nest. The water turned all the colours of the rainbow and the trapped goblins whizzed around and around in the bubbly liquid.

POP! Without warning a goblin shot out from the chute, somersaulted through the air and landed at Polly's feet.

POP! Without warning, another one followed.

POP! POP! POP! POP! POP! That was another five.

POP! POP! POPPITY-POP-POP POP!
That was absolutely loads of them.

Soon all the goblins had been spat out on to the pavement. There they sat, dazed and blinking in the sunlight.

But somehow they looks different, thought Polly. *Where's all their fins an' spikes an' claws?*

Because the goblins were goblins no longer.

They were children with rosy cheeks and happy laughing faces.

'Thank you, Polly!' laughed a boy called Terry, who had once been Captain Ankles. 'You saved us!'

'I used to be Livermonk, who burped ever so much,' said a tiny girl called Caroline. 'But now look at me – I'm back to good old Caroline. The Fruit Chew of Babylon has made everything all right!'

'What the grapefruit's a-goin' on?' said Polly in amazement, as the rest of the heroes rushed up, led by David Casserole, the Town Mayor.

'Well done, Polly!' he beamed. 'You've found the three hundred children who ran away in September!'

Chapter 13
The Truth About It All

'See,' laughed Terry. 'I'm not Captain Ankles at all. These fins and spikes and claws and things – they're not real. They're just costumes!'

'But why did you behaves so bad an' pretend to be goblins?' asked Polly in confusion.

'I'm ashamed to say it's because we were horrible naughty children,' said Caroline, stepping forward with a red face. 'We didn't like going to school one little bit!'

'And one afternoon the teachers made us be in a pathetic school play called *300 Goblins Standing Around Doing Nothing*,' said Alex (who used to be the goblin known as Big Steve).

'Only we didn't want to,' continued a tall girl called Vicky (previously Soupdog).

'So we ran away to Goblin Mountain, still in our costumes,' said Eric (Yak Triangle).

'And we ran amuck and lived like savages, and we acted so wild that eventually we forgot we had ever been children at all,' confessed Brian (Wippy).

'And one day Mr Gum and Billy William spied us,' said Veronica (Oink Balloon), 'and they thought we really *were* goblins. And by then we had forgotten all our lessons or even how to speak properly. So we just joined their army for a spiteful laugh.'

'But now the Fruit Chew of Babylon has made us understand how important school is,' said Terry. 'Otherwise we might end up like Mr Gum or Billy William, who never did learn better. But please don't make us go back to our old school, it was just no good!'

'Children,' said Alan Taylor, who had been listening carefully. 'Which school were you at?'

'Doctor No-Fun's School Of Boredom, of course,' replied Alex.

'Yes, I've heard about Doctor No-Fun's,' sighed Alan Taylor. 'They're very old-fashioned there. But at 𝕾𝖆𝖎𝖓𝖙 𝕻𝖙𝖊𝖗𝖔𝖉𝖆𝖈𝖙𝖞𝖑'𝖘 𝕾𝖈𝖍𝖔𝖔𝖑 𝕱𝖔𝖗 𝕿𝖍𝖊 𝕻𝖔𝖔𝖗, we believe in teaching children about the natural world and letting them do paintings about how they're really feeling inside.'

'Oh, we'd like to go there ever so much!' chorused the children.

'I'm sorry,' said Alan Taylor sadly. 'There are no available places.'

The children's faces fell.

'Only joking!' cried the gingerbread prankster, his electric muscles whirring merrily. 'Come with me, you will be my first ever pupils!' And away he jigged up the hill, the children skipping happily after him.

'Look, children,' Polly heard him say as they disappeared from view. 'That tall brown thing is known as a "tree".'

After that, everyone congratulated everyone else
and all the townsfolk were full of joy and
merriment. Well, nearly all of them.

'You were going to put me in that machine,
weren't you?' said Jonathan Ripples, tapping
Martin Launderette on the shoulder with a
chubby finger.

'Yes I was,' admitted Martin Launderette,
trying to look ashamed. 'But . . . um . . . now the

Fruit Chew of Babylon has taught me the error of my ways – '

'Forget it, skinny,' said Jonathan Ripples sternly. 'You are SO getting sat on.'

'Everything's back to normal,' smiled Polly, looking on as Martin Launderette was squashed into oblivion. 'But hold on – what abouts Mr Gum an' Billy?'

'Don't you worry about them,' said Friday, tapping his nose. 'I left them at Boaster's Hill. They promised to wait for me to come back with something to tie them up. And look,' he said proudly. 'I've just bought a nice strong rope – why, Polly whatever's wrong?'

'Them two scruffers done tricked you,' said Polly, shaking her head sadly. 'I bets you anythin' they've run off by now.'

'Nonsense,' said Friday confidently.

'They'll still be there. After all, Mr Gum and Billy William are very trustworthy men. They – oh,' he said, realising he'd been fooled by master criminals. 'Oops.'

'Never mind, Friday,' said Polly. 'The important thing is, Lamonic Bibber's OK and it's time for a big pig blowout feast!'

So off they skipped to the town square, to find the feast already underway. And what a turnout! Nearly everyone was there – Old Granny, the little girl called Peter, Marvellous Marvin, the retired wrestler. . . Beany McLeany, who loved things that rhymed, was having a chat about a cat with a bloke in a hat, and Jake the dog was helping Mrs Lovely to make sweets by licking up the bits that fell on the floor. And when Mrs Lovely's back was turned, he was helping by making bits fall on the floor on purpose.

'But where's the Spirit of the Rainbow?' said Polly, looking around. 'He should be here enjoyin' the fun an' showin' everyone what a winner he is!'

'That honest lad cares not for rewards and fame, little miss,' nodded Friday wisely. 'And that is why he is the Spirit of the Rainbow instead of a snooker player or something.'

Oh, well. I'll tell you who did turn up, though. That rabbit from the mountainside. It hopped into Polly's skirt pocket and there it sat for the rest of the day, drinking a carton of apple juice. Oh, and Alan Taylor came back down the hill with his new pupils. And they'd already done loads of amazing paintings showing how they really felt inside, and everyone clapped.

'Good work, children,' said Alan Taylor and he rewarded them all with tiny gold stars and ten 'bonus Alan points' each.

And from Polly's skirt pocket the rabbit watched the whole happy affair. *All's well that*

ends well, its bright green eyes seemed to say.
Mmm, this is nice apple juice.

And the laughter and the capering continued on,
and none laughed louder or capered harder than
Polly and her good friend, Friday O'Leary. For
though their legs were tired from their long
journey, their hearts were bursting like joyful

apricots to be back where they belonged.

'Look, Frides,' exclaimed Polly at length. 'The snow's a-meltin'. An' the sun's comin' out proud as you please an' soon all the ice cream vans will come out of hibernation!'

'I do believe you're right,' said Friday. 'What an adventure it's been. Tell you what,' he nodded, getting out his blue guitar. 'This calls for a song!'

'You better hurry it up then,' said Polly. 'I gots a feelin' we're nearly out of time.'

'Time, little miss?' laughed Friday. 'Why, we've got all the time in the

THE END

Hello again.

You know, Polly and Friday aren't the only ones who have adventures in Lamonic Bibber. Old Granny, the oldest woman in town, has been known to get up to some pretty wild stuff too. And while all that goblin malarkey was going on, O.G. was having quite an adventure of her own . . .

Old Granny's Cardigan Adventure

One cold winter's day, Old Granny awoke in her big brass bed from before the War, had a little sip of sherry from the bottle she always kept by the bedside, and got up. She brushed her false teeth with her false toothbrush, and had a little sip of sherry from the bottle she kept in her bathroom cabinet from before the War. Then she went downstairs, had some cornflakes, and turned on her old TV from before the War. Actually, a lot of things in Old Granny's house were from before the War, I think I'll stop mentioning that now.

Then Old Granny had a sip of sherry from the bottle she always kept down the back of the armchair. Then she had a sip of sherry from a little bottle she always kept hidden in the first bottle.

Then she phoned her brother, Old Danny, on her huge old-fashioned black telephone.

'Hello, Old Danny,' said Old Granny. 'How are you?'

'Old,' said Old Danny.

'Me too,' said Old Granny. 'Great, isn't it?'

'Yes, and I'm always having adventures,' replied Old Danny. 'For instance, this morning I found a penny on the kitchen floor. And last week, I found a penny on the kitchen floor.'

'Perhaps it was the same penny,' said Old Granny.

'Perhaps,' laughed Old Danny. 'What an exciting mystery it all is!'

'I haven't had an adventure for ages,' said Old Granny wistfully. 'The last proper adventure I had was in 1978 when I joined that punk rock band. Do you remember?'

'Oh, yes,' said Old Danny. 'Rancid Vomit.

What a great band that was. I've got all your records, especially since I'm your brother.'

'Yes,' sighed Old Granny. 'Well, I'd better go now, Old Danny, because you live in Australia, don't you? And you're asleep in bed.'

'That's right,' said Old Danny. 'Call me if you have any adventures. Bye.'

Well, Old Granny sat there for some time, having a bit of a daydream. After a while, she decided to go out to buy some milk, a bag of those special horrible sweets that only old people are allowed to buy and some more sherry – and that's when the adventure began.

'I can't find my cardigan!' she said in amazement. 'Where can it be?'

My goodness, what an adventure! Old Granny must have looked for that cardigan for nearly three minutes! But finally she found it. It was lying on the kitchen floor.

'Just wait till Old Danny hears about this!' chuckled Old Granny, picking up the phone once more. 'He'll have to call me Old CARDIGRANNY!'

And he did.

THE END

'Your brain's too small for your head!'

Hello. Andy Stanton here, announcing the winner of the world famous 'Make Up An Insult For Mr Gum To Say' Competition. Catchy title, huh? Well, no, but anyway, the winner is . . . Maya Lingam! Well done, Miss Lingam!

You can see Mr Gum saying the winning phrase in Chapter 9, but in the meantime here are some facts about Maya herself. They are all true, except for one which I made up. See if you can spot the imposter:

1 Maya was born in 1997!

2 Maya's favourite colour is purple!

3 Maya doesn't like onions!

4 Maya's favourite Mr Gum character is Monsieur Bellybutton!

5 Maya can change into any sort of animal just by thinking about it!

BYE!

Andy Stanton

About the Illustrator

David Tazzyman lives in South London with his girlfriend, Melanie, and their son, Stanley. He grew up in Leicester, studied illustration at Manchester Metropolitan University and then travelled around Asia for three years before moving to London in 1997. He likes football, cricket, biscuits, music and drawing. He still dislikes celery.

About the Author

Andy Stanton lives in North London. He studied English at Oxford but they kicked him out. He has been a film script reader, a cartoonist, an NHS lackey and lots of other things. He has many interests, but best of all he likes cartoons, books and music (even jazz). One day he'd like to live in New York or Berlin or one of those places because he's got fantasies of bohemia. His favourite expression is 'Rumble it up, Uncle Charlie!' and his favourite word is 'platypus'. This is his eighth book.

Surf the Net in Style! at ...

www.egmont.co.uk/mrgum

Why do exercise and healthy outdoors pursuits
when you can sit all hunched up in front of a tiny
computer screen, laughing your little face off
at the all-new, all-fantastic, all-bonkers
OFFICIAL MR GUM OFFICIAL WEBSITE?!

Yes, no lie, it's true! The OFFICIAL
MR GUM OFFICIAL WEBSITE features:

- *Things!*
- *Games!*
- *Photos* of the author with beard
  and without!
- *News* about Mr Gum books and other stuff!
- *Loud noises!*
- *Words* like 'YANKLE', 'BLITTLER' and 'FLOINK'!
- *Crafty Tom* – the Tyrannosaurus rex
  with a heart of gold!*

You'll never need to go outdoors again!

*Actual website may not include Crafty Tom